Rosalie's
Big Dream

Ginette Anfousse

Illustrated by Marisol Sarrazin
Translated by Linda Gaboriau

RAGWEED
THE ISLAND PUBLISHER

10 9 8 7 6 5 4 3 2 1

Cover and book illustrations: Marisol Sarrazin
Printed and bound in Canada by: Webcom

*Ragweed Press acknowledges the generous support of the Canada
Council.*

Published by:
Ragweed Press
P.O. Box 2023
Charlottetown, P.E.I.
Canada, C1A 7N7

Canadian Cataloguing in Publication Data
Anfousse, Ginette, 1944-

[Grand rêve de Rosalie. English]

Rosalie's big dream

Translation of: Le grand rêve de Rosalie.
ISBN 0-921556-52-7 (pbk.). — ISBN 0-921556-53-5 (bound)

I. Sarrazin, Marisol, 1965- II. Title. III. Title: Grand rêve de
Rosalie. English.

PS8551.N42G7213 1995 jC843'.54 C95-950022-7
PZ7.A64Ro 1995

To Guillaume Lacoste,
with many thanks for your
invaluable advice.

Contents

The problem with my best friend is her holy hopping horrible intelligence!

Really! Julie Morin can add as fast as an electronic calculator. She never makes spelling mistakes. And she knows almost all the definitions in the dictionary by heart.

She knows the names of all the animals in Africa, all the fish in the Pacific, every make of car and the best rock groups. She knows the Chinese horoscope, the signs of the Zodiac and, of course, every brand of computer.

I suppose it's because she knows everything that everyone assumes that she's always right. So not only has the whole school known for ages that Julie is best at EVERYTHING ... but, as of this morning, everyone knows that Rosalie Dansereau, the best at NOTHING, has a BIG DREAM.

It was a holy hopping bad idea to have told everything to Julie! A really holy hopping horrible bad idea!

Chapter 1
A Poor Gemini-Horse!

In fact, I didn't intend to tell Julie Morin everything. I really wanted to confide in Pierre-Yves Hamel. But my Viking hero didn't have two seconds to listen to me last weekend. He was too busy repainting all thirteen doors in his parents' apartment.

Poor Pierre-Yves! Thirteen bottle-green doors to be painted white. And since his dear mother insisted upon three coats of paint — and each door had two sides — my hero had to paint seventy-eight doors in all!

On Saturday night, I almost told my seven aunts everything. But before announcing to Aunt Alice, Aunt Beatrice, Aunt Colette, Aunt Diane, Aunt Elisabeth, Aunt Florence, and Aunt Gertrude that there was a superstar in the family ... I decided to rehearse a bit more.

So I held my tongue for the entire weekend. Everything was fine until I arrived in the schoolyard this morning. That's when it all started. I mean the holy horrible uncontrollable need to tell everything to someone and right away.

The minute I spotted my best friend, I took two seconds to make sure the quarters I had glued to the soles of my shoes were still in place. I had stuck them on with *Crazy Glue* the night before.

"Don't move," I shouted from the other side of the schoolyard. "I have something to show you. You have to tell me what you think, O.K., Julie Morin?"

I took a deep breath, braced myself,

than launched into four rat-a-tap-taps, two pirouettes and a dozen other tap steps.

Then, I waited. I waited for my best friend to stop staring at me with that look of hers — the look of someone who's always so sure of herself.

"What's the big idea, Rosalie Dansereau?" she finally said. "You look like an electric grasshopper that just got bitten by a bee!"

Ouch! Sometimes my friend Julie is a real pain! But this time, I didn't get upset.

"That's because you don't know anything about tap-dancing ... Otherwise, you would have recognized the grand finale from the best movie the super GREAT American dancer, Fred Astaire, ever made."

To convince her, I added that I had secretly watched my Aunt Colette's video cassette eighty-two times. I was sure that would make her eat her words. But once again, Julie was the one who made me eat my words.

As she usually does to make her point, she started rattling off names — the names of all the tap-dancing, jazz ballet and rap films she'd seen on television. Then she suggested that I forget the triple time steps, the wings and the pullbacks — steps that were obviously too difficult for me.

She was talking gobbledygook, as far as I was concerned. But you don't always have to understand to get hot under the collar.

Finally, to make her shut up, I yelled that she should wait until I had some real tap shoes ... then she'd see the difference.

And without realizing that a holy hopping huge crowd had gathered round us, I announced that I was no longer going to be a veterinarian, but ... THE BEST VIDEO-CLIP TAP-DANCER in North America!

I actually was thinking about Europe and Asia, too. But I didn't say so. I didn't say so because my supposedly best friend had just acted like my holy hopping worst enemy.

"You're not the right type to become a star, Rosalie Dansereau!" she declared.

And without taking a breath or missing a beat, she continued, "I know your type, you're a Gemini-Horse. Like all

Gemini-Horses, you dream in technicolour. You can't accept criticism. And worst of all, you're stubborn! Besides, in all my Chinese astrology books, they say that Gemini-Horses should live alone! And that they should avoid crowds! In other words, Rosalie Dansereau, you should take care of animals."

And as if it weren't enough to have your friend confront you with the holy hopping horrible facts, I heard a baby from grade two repeat after her like a parrot, "Julie Morin is right ... We liked you better when you wanted to take care of sick cats and dogs and pigeons!"

Then I saw at least thirty people nod their heads ... letting me know that my dream was super, super, hyper dumb.

I turned on my heels. I walked into the school and ran to hide in the girls' room. I had a good cry, sitting there in one of the stalls. Then I tried with all my might to tear off the six quarters I'd glued to the soles of my shoes with *Crazy Glue*. I couldn't get them off.

Instead, I stuck four super bandaids on top of them. Aunt Alice always slips a box of bandaids into my schoolbag. "Just in case!" as she would say. I stepped out of the stall and went to look at myself in the mirror.

First, I tried to flatten my wild Javanese Indian curls. I tucked my T-shirt into my jeans. I screwed up my nerve, pushed the door open and headed down the hall. But before I had taken six steps, I heard the principal call to me from the other end of the hallway.

"You'd do anything to attract attention, wouldn't you, Rosalie Dansereau!"

That's when I realized that the four super bandaids had not solved my problem! My shoes still made an unbelievable racket!

Finally, long before the bell rang, I went to sit at my desk. I slouched down into my seat, wishing I could disappear.

I spent the rest of the day trying to avoid everyone. Even Marise Cormier, my other best friend. Even Pierre-Yves Hamel, my hero.

As soon as I got home, around four o'clock, I grabbed my cat Charcoal and went straight up to my room.

My heart was as heavy as a ton of bricks, I was so mad at my ex-best friend.

I didn't know anything about the Chinese horoscope, and hardly anything about horoscopes in general. But I couldn't see myself spending my entire life all alone, repairing animals' broken legs.

A little while later, as I sat there patting Charcoal, I thought about my real father

19

and my real mother in their heaven. I suddenly realized what a terrible mistake my mother had made by giving birth to me in the springtime. She should have given birth to me in the fall or in the winter, or a few years earlier or a few years later.

I realized that I could have been a Leo-Dragon who would have never lost her parents in an airplane crash! A Leo-Dragon who could live surrounded by people. A Leo-Dragon who could become a real superstar and earn the applause of a thousand million spectators!

The more I thought about what I could have become, and would never be, the madder I was at the calendar, at the stars in general, and at Julie Morin in particular.

Finally, I told myself that even if I should abandon the idea of becoming one of the world's greatest stars ... I could still become the best tap-dancer on St. Joseph Boulevard.

I put Charcoal down in his basket and I

quietly began to brush the floor, click my heels and tap my feet.

I really loved to hear the rat-a-tap-tap fill the air. It made me feel as if I had twenty legs, eight hundred toes and a pair of wings.

I raised my head high, shook my Javanese Indian curls and began to practice the grand finale from the best movie Fred Astaire ever made.

The more I practiced, the higher I could jump and the farther I could slide. The rat-a-tap-taps echoed louder and faster all around me. This was totally different from my secret rehearsals in my stocking feet over the weekend.

Now I was sure, no matter what Julie Morin said, that I would not only impress the whole street, but the entire solar system.

I was whirling around like a carefree sparrow when the door to my room flew open.

My seven aunts were standing behind the door. I froze in my tracks. And so did they.

The carefree sparrow came crashing down when she heard Aunt Beatrice sound just like Julie Morin: "What's the big idea, Rosalie Dansereau?"

Then Aunt Gertrude, like an echo: "Really, poison, what is the idea?"

When they surrounded me, sighing and clucking their tongues, TSK! TSK!, I got really fed up and replied, "The idea is that I'm not allowed to move a muscle in this house! Not even in my own room!"

My seven aunts stared at me and rolled their eyes, the way they always do when they imagine that they're my real mothers and think that I'm exaggerating.

"Tap-shoes are all very well, chickadee," Aunt Alice finally muttered, "but ... I just found a layer of plaster in my pie crust."

I was just about to open my mouth and protest that she was exaggerating a bit herself, when my seven aunts attacked my shoes. Like seven magpies, they all started to chatter and cackle and complain.

I had to put up with terrible sarcasm and the kind of teasing that a teenager in a normal family would never have to endure.

Aunt Gertrude swore she thought a jackhammer had been set up on the roof. Aunt Diane talked about heavy metal cassettes stuck between the two floors. For Aunt Elisabeth, the Canadian armed forces had chosen our basement for their manoeuvres. And Aunt Beatrice dared talk about a herd of wild elephants destroying her living room.

Apparently, there were limits to what they could bear, limits to the decibel level their eardrums could tolerate.

Finally, long before they began their usual lecture on today's youth, I made a decision. I decided to play dead so I wouldn't have to listen to them.

Under the horrified gaze of my seven aunts, I quietly took off my shoes. I walked over to my bed and lay down on my quilt. I stared at the ceiling for a while. Then I

closed my eyes. I was fully prepared to stay
that way for eternity.

My little performance must have really
impressed them because within ten minutes
they had all left my room, as silent as sunfish
and reasonably upset.

Even Charcoal, my cat, began to sniff at my eyelids and miaow. The poor kitty must have thought that Rosalie Dansereau had turned into a statue.

To reassure him, I scratched the spot behind his ears where I always manage to start his little purr motor. After a while, Charcoal fell asleep.

I was just about to fall asleep myself when I heard the phone ring.

I almost leapt out of bed, ran down the hall and pounced on the phone — but instead I closed my eyes as soon as I recognized Aunt Alice's footsteps.

She hesitated for a moment behind the door. Then she came in. She hesitated again, before coming over to whisper in my ear, "It's Pierre-Yves on the phone ... Did you hear me, chickadee? Don't talk too long. Supper is ready and there's blueberry pie for dessert."

Even though blueberry pie is my favourite dessert, even though I really wanted to talk to my hero and tell him how hard it is to have the whole world against you ... I played statue again. I still refused to say a word or budge an inch.

Aunt Alice walked around in circles for a few seconds, then finally left the room sighing, "How can anyone so young make herself suffer so much?"

I found her words a bit strange. In the first place, I wasn't suffering. And why would anyone think that age had anything to do with pain?

I never once set foot out of my room that entire evening, not even to eat, or brush my teeth or wash. It wasn't until after ten-thirty, when my aunts were all asleep, that I picked up Charcoal in one hand and my tap shoes in the other. Then, without making a sound, I crept down the stairs.

I rushed to the back of the kitchen and unlocked the door that leads to the alleyway.

With my heart in my throat, I walked to the corner of Garnier Street in my stocking feet.

The street was super deserted and super scarey, but high above the rooftops, a huge, round moon was shining as bright as a movie spotlight.

I put Charcoal down on the pavement, slipped on my shoes and started to tap my toes and heels.

What a fabulous feeling of freedom!

It was fabulous having the stars as spotlights! And the alleyway as my stage! And the sheds as amplifiers!

The sound reverberated from side to side, ahead of me and behind me. This was the ideal place to rehearse! The ideal place … until an uncivilised neighbour shouted from a third floor balcony that he was going to call the police.

I shouted back that the alleyway belonged to everyone. And I went on dancing.

I went on until Charcoal received, courtesy of the same uncivilised neighbour, the equivalent of a bathtub full of icy water on his back.

At that point, I had to beat a hasty retreat. My cat was growling and miaowing loud enough to alert every neighbourhood in Montreal.

I had to tickle the spot behind his ears like crazy to get his little purr motor started.

Charcoal finally calmed down, and I headed home incognito.

I crept back up the stairs and into my room, pretty exhausted and, most of all, super, super depressed.

Chapter 3
The Worst Scorpio-Snake

Now I know why all great stars wear dark glasses. It's an old habit, a habit they developed, like me, before they were really famous. Back when everyone made fun of them.

For the past three days, I've been rehearsing my grand finale at school, without saying a word to anyone. For three days, hidden behind my sunglasses, I've listened to people say the worst holy hopping horrible things behind my back.

They whisper that I think I'm different,

that I think I'm something else. The truth is that it's hard to be like everybody else when you spend your days off in a corner on your own.

Anyway, in order to make the biggest dream in my life come true, I'm willing to let all of St. Mary's School make fun of me. I'll put up with Marco Tifo shrugging his shoulders, Marise Cormier giggling her head off, and Julie Morin looking superior.

The only thing that bothers me a bit is Pierre-Yves Hamel's desperate glances. Since I no longer feel like sharing my dream with anybody, I've been avoiding my hero like the plague, and he's beginning to look at me as if I had a hole in my noggin.

This afternoon, on the way back from recess, I realized that I was right not to trust other people. It's hard to believe, but, I swear, someone had left a real anonymous letter on top of my books, inside my desk. The letter was printed in block letters and signed: "Someone who cares about you."

Without blinking an eye, I slipped the paper into my math notebook. Then I waited until quarter to four before transferring the note to my schoolbag.

Actually, it didn't say much. A few comments on my overall attitude and the name and address of the best dance school in Quebec.

I didn't have a minute's doubt about who wrote the letter. But to make absolutely sure, I checked my dictionary and the telephone book to see if there were any spelling mistakes. Since there were no mistakes, I was surer than ever that the person who cared about me so much was Julie Morin.

I crumpled up the letter and threw it into my wastepaper basket. Then I finally had a good idea — I decided to pay a little visit to Aunt Florence's room.

Auntie Flo is my vegetarian aunt, the one who spends her time standing on her head, her legs in the air, practicing yoga.

She is the aunt who's most concerned about my spiritual welfare.

Without really knowing why, I was almost sure I'd find what I was looking for in her room.

I knocked on her door loudly and went in. As usual, Auntie Flo was super, hyper concentrated. She was staring at a crystal pyramid and muttering strange words.

She was concentrating so hard, she didn't hear or see a thing, even though, for at least a half hour, I turned her desk and her bookcase upside down and inside out.

Before long, I was back in my own room with the best collection of books on the Chinese horoscope, and on the horoscope in general, anyone could ever hope to find.

I spread the pile of books out on my bed and I read everything, absolutely everything, there was on Scorpio-Snakes.

Scorpio-Snake! Those are Julie Morin's astrological signs!

Two hours later, I had memorized all,

absolutely all, of my ex-best friend's weak points!!!

When I sat down at my desk, I didn't realize it was going to take me the entire

evening, and a good part of the night, to write, correct, cut and paste the longest anonymous letter without a single mistake ever written.

Finally, around three o'clock in the morning, when there was no longer a sliver of moon in the sky, I dragged myself over to my bed. I crept under my quilt, incognito, and fell asleep, pretty exhausted, but no longer the least bit depressed.

Chapter 4
Like Fred Astaire

The next morning, I had the absolutely worst time dragging myself out of bed. I stumbled off to school with my lunch, my tap shoes, my dark glasses and my super anonymous letter.

I immediately rushed up to the fourth floor and slipped the letter into my best friend's desk. Then I went back downstairs and sauntered into the schoolyard, looking innocent.

Then I did what I'd been doing for the past four days: while everyone else was laughing, fooling around and talking, I went over to the school wall and began to work.

Compared to the other days, not so many kids gathered to watch and make fun of me behind my back. I guess they were getting used to my pirouettes. My tap-dancing routine didn't seem to bother anyone anymore. I don't know why, but this time it wasn't easy to keep tapping my feet until the bell rang.

All that morning, I kept my eye on Julie Morin. When I walked into the classroom, I saw her open her desk, then read my super anonymous letter. My ten-page letter contained enough unpleasant things about Scorpio-Snakes to drive anyone up the wall! But Julie Morin acted as if she couldn't care less about everything I had written.

Suddenly, I remembered that Scorpio-Snakes are still waters that run deep! That they never let their emotions show! And, according to Aunt Florence's books, they prefer to plot their revenge in secret.

That was when I realized that Julie Morin would be merciless. I didn't dare take my eyes off her. That was easy, since my seat in class is directly behind hers. As I sat there staring at her neck, I also realized that snakes can hypnotize us from behind.

To prove it, I was actually dreaming that a boa constrictor had swallowed me whole when Miss Lessing, our English teacher, startled me by yelling that her classroom wasn't a dormitory and that I should go to bed earlier!

Everyone started laughing and I knew that, in the future, I'd better avoid looking at my best friend's neck.

Around noon, I went down to the cafeteria. I sat down at a table all by myself and began nibbling on my peanut butter sandwich, my celery sticks, my carrot sticks, my apple-pear and my half-dozen little yellow plums.

From behind my dark glasses, not only

could I observe the comings and goings of the entire school, but I could also keep an eye on the table where all my ex-friends were eating.

I was sucking on the pit of my last plum when I saw Julie Morin push back her chair, stand up like the Queen of England and walk across the cafeteria ... only to come and sit right beside me.

I tried to act as if I hadn't even noticed her. But I had the awful bad luck of GULP! swallowing my holy hopping horrible plum pit. Suddenly, I turned as red as a beet. And even though I was coughing, choking, suffocating ... nobody, absolutely nobody, rushed over to save my life.

In the end, it was my ex-best friend who took advantage of the situation and finally made me spit up the pit by banging on my back.

I'd barely had time to recover when she declared, as if it were a national emergency, "You don't have to choke to death ... I just wanted to know the exact time of your birth."

Like the world's worst scatterbrain, I answered, "I was born at Maisonneuve Hospital, on a Wednesday, at exactly noon."

And stretching the truth a lot, I added, "Like Leonardo da Vinci, Michael Jackson, Madonna and Mitsou, at least four presidents of the United States, Mother Teresa, Marie Curie, Alexander Graham Bell, Albert Einstein and Fred Astaire, of course."

I don't know why, but I expected her to respond with a flood of allusions and a bunch of insinuations.

Instead, she simply muttered, "Obviously, the exact time of birth can make a big difference ..."

Then she stood up again like the Queen of England, and without even mentioning the anonymous letter or anything else, she went back to sit at the far end of the cafeteria with Marise Cormier and Marco Tifo.

It took me a while to understand. And

to realize that I had talked too much. I mean, I shouldn't have told her the exact time of my birth and all that. They are such opportunists, such calculating, plotting, jealous sneaks — you can't trust Scorpio-Snakes!

Later on, somewhere between three o'clock and three-thirty, since nothing interesting had happened all afternoon, I fell asleep again, face down on my geography book.

This time it was the school principal who shook me and told me that school was over for the day! That everyone else had gone home! And that I should take advantage of the weekend to catch up on my sleep!

I dragged myself home, fully intending to take a nap before supper. But that's not how things worked out.

As I arrived home, I saw Aunt Beatrice spying on me from behind the living room curtains. I understood immediately that Sergeant Celery wanted to get something off

her chest. But what? I was sure I'd made my
bed before leaving that morning.

The second I stepped inside, she or-
dered me to take off my shoes and follow
her, down on my hands and knees like a holy
horrible chihuahua, up and down every hall
in the house. She wanted to make sure that
I not only saw but counted the four hundred
and thirty-two little marks my six quarters
had left on her hardwood floors.

That was her way of telling me that I wouldn't be allowed to wear my tap shoes in the house anymore.

I grabbed the pair of running shoes she was holding as if they were a dangerous weapon, and I ran up to my room. Then I slammed the door with all my might, just to make it clear that I didn't agree.

After that, I wasn't the least bit sleepy. I paced around my room, back and forth and round in circles. I felt so alone, so horribly alone. I even considered abandoning my big dream for good.

But before giving up, I thought there must be someone, somewhere, who could share my dream. Someone for whom tap-dancing meant more than marks on a hardwood floor, more than silly antics or unwelcome noise in the night.

Then I remembered the anonymous letter. With my heart beating furiously, I fished through my wastepaper basket. I finally found the holy hopping horror of a letter under an old banana peel. Then I crept down the hall and dialled the number of the so-called best dance school in Quebec.

Somebody answered immediately. But after the phone call, I swear, I felt more discouraged than ever.

First of all, to find someone, some-where, who could share my big dream, I would have to take not only one tap-dancing class a week, but a ballet class as well! They claim it's good for your flexibility. And real tap shoes, with real taps and everything, cost at least a hundred dollars!

And worst of all, they were going to put me in the beginners' class, even though I told them over and over again that I'd been rehearsing Fred Astaire's grand finale like a maniac for at least six days!

When I hung up the phone, I realized that the best dance school in Quebec was not for me! That wasn't where I'd find my tap-dancing soul mate! And if I really wanted to dream a bit, I should follow my principal's advice and lie down on my bed and sleep for real!

Chapter 5
No Friends, No Hero

I spent the worst holy hopping horrible weekend of my entire life.

First of all, Charcoal went off smooching day and night with Pierre-Yves' Kimmicat.

Then every single one of the forty-six phone calls this weekend was for one of my aunts.

And to top it all off, the huge full moon as bright as a movie spotlight disappeared on Saturday evening, drowned in a sea of dark clouds, a sea as immobile as the parking lot at a shopping centre in the middle of the night.

Finally, since it was raining cats and dogs in the alleyway behind St. Joseph Boulevard — and I wasn't allowed to wear my tap shoes in the house anymore — I spent two days standing guard over the mail-box.

I would have loved to catch Julie Morin in the act. But I guess my ex-best friend was waiting to take her revenge when we were back at school on Monday.

Never have I been so eager to go back to school on a Monday morning. I've never been in such a hurry to slip my hand into my desk. I wanted to read Julie Morin's second anonymous letter. Then it would be my turn to act as if I couldn't care less. I could hardly wait to get home that night and compose my second answer, a thousand times worse than the first.

But … after spending the worst weekend in my entire life, I also spent the worst holy hopping horrible Monday in my entire life.

There was nothing in my desk. Nothing stuck between the pages of my fifteen books. Nothing in my notebooks. Nothing in my pigeon-hole. Nothing in the pocket of my gym outfit.

Nothing, absolutely nothing, anywhere. Really, I'm sure. I searched high and low, inside and out.

So I had to do exactly what I'd done the week before — go off in a corner, hidden behind my dark glasses, and rehearse my tap-dancing routine like a maniac, facing the school wall. And I had to spend another long day without saying a word to anyone.

I'm afraid that was getting easier and easier to do, since hardly a soul was speaking to me these days. And I was beginning to understand why.

Ever since Julie Morin had found out the exact time of my birth, I was sure she had been repeating the most holy horrible abominable things about me to anyone who would listen.

Scorpio-Snakes are so jealous! Uncontrollably jealous, according to all of Auntie Flo's books! I was also sure that Marise Cormier and Marco Tifo were easily influenced! That's why they hadn't dared call me!

Most of all, I was sure that was why Pierre-Yves Hamel no longer sent his desperate looks my way. It was almost as if he had completely forgotten about me.

When I got home from school, I had another idea. An idea of how I could find out just how much Pierre-Yves Hamel had allowed himself to be influenced. My idea was so terrible, so horrible, that my heart felt heavier than ten tons of bricks just thinking about it.

Imagine how heartbroken I felt when, an hour later, I filled a large paper bag with everything my hero had ever given me. I'm talking about his sweatshirt, his *Swatch* watch, his four love letters, his postcard from the States, his two books on windsurfing and his photograph.

I started to cry and cry as I wrote an explanatory note on the bag:

> *Dear Pierre-Yves,*
> *Since people have convinced you I am not the girl you thought I was, I am returning your belongings. I'm sure that your sweatshirt will look better on the girl you're thinking about now.*
> And I signed: *Rosalie Dansereau.*

I was much too sad to tell him how much I loved him anyway, much too sad to deliver the package in person. So I put the bag down in front of his door, rang the bell and took off.

I came home and, I swear, I didn't feel like doing anything — I didn't feel like crying, or studying, or watching TV. I didn't even feel like dancing in the alley or in my stocking feet.

I stopped living and waited for the

phone to ring. I was waiting for my hero to react.

Once again, I waited in vain. Around eight o'clock, I realized that I no longer existed for anybody, and that, in addition to

having lost all my friends, I had really and truly lost the love of my life.

I grabbed my running shoes and spent the rest of the evening furiously trying to tear the holy horrible quarters off the soles. I ended up gluing six felt patches over them, using the same holy hopping horrible *Crazy Glue.* Then I finally crept into bed. I still wonder how I managed to fall asleep.

Chapter 6
Tomatoes and Rotten Eggs

Tuesday, I went back to school reluctantly. As I walked down the sidewalk on St. Joseph Boulevard, I no longer heard the rat-a-tap-tap that I loved so much.

I no longer had twenty legs, eight hundred toes and a pair of wings. Instead, I felt as if I was crawling silently through a tunnel full of ugly, slimy, disgusting, dangerous bugs.

When I reached the schoolyard, I went and sat against the wall where I usually practiced. As I waited for the bell to ring, I studied the little ants that were circling round my feet in single file.

During the afternoon recess, I did exactly the same thing. But since there's a limit to how long you can watch ants crawl between your toes, I soon raised my head.

I raised my head, and I regretted it. Standing directly in front of me was a group of students who were staring at me as if I had leprosy or the plague, or some holy hopping horror of a contagious disease.

I swear, it was as if, after performing on the biggest stage in the world, people were throwing tomatoes, potatoes, turnips and rotten eggs at me.

I almost felt like screaming, biting and scratching. But instead I acted like a holy horrible Scorpio-Snake. I put my dark glasses on, I tossed my Javanese Indian curls harder than ever, and I stood up, my nose in the air, like Julie Morin or the Queen of England.

That's how I crossed the entire schoolyard.

Then I walked through the gate and, without even looking over my shoulder, I turned down the street.

I walked to the corner of Garnier Street. Then I started to run, and I ran all the way home.

It wasn't until I was walking up the front steps that I remembered it was still Tuesday, and that, by some inexplicable stroke of bad luck, it was still Sergeant Celery's day off! I didn't have the courage to enter the house.

I preferred to wander up and down every side street in Montreal. Around four o'clock, I decided to go home.

For once, Aunt Beatrice wasn't hiding behind the curtains in the living room, waiting for me to arrive. She was crouching, l swear, like a bird of prey behind the front door.

It didn't take long for me to realize that the principal had called. So before Sergeant Celery even had time to tell me how super awful it was to miss school without good reason, I clenched my fists and told her how urgent it was for us to move. Pack up! Change streets! Change neighbours! Change friends! Change neighbourhoods!

Aunt Beatrice has no imagination at all. She simply sent me straight to my room so that I could calm down. It was a silly idea, because I wasn't the least bit calmer two hours later, when I heard someone knocking at my door.

"Sweetness … it's only me," a voice murmured.

I immediately recognized Aunt Colette's singsong voice. I was positive that Aunt Beatrice had sent her ahead as a scout.

It wasn't hard to figure out why! As everyone in the family knows, Aunt Colette's big dream is to become the greatest actress of modern times, and everyone still thinks that my big dream is to become the best tap-dancer in North America. So Aunt

Beatrice preferred to send Aunt Colette to explain things to me.

But I hadn't spoken to anyone for days. I had so many things to get off my chest, and I felt so angry and so sad, that I yanked open my door and threw myself into her arms! Aunt Colette probably wasn't expecting that. Then, believe me, she had no choice but to sit down and listen to me.

She even had tears in her eyes when I told her that I had lost all my friends! That the whole school was making fun of me! That nobody at St. Mary's School even spoke to me anymore! And that not only had I received dozens of anonymous letters, but dozens and dozens of pails of water had been poured over my head!

She hugged me really tight when I told her how proud I was of her — proud to see her almost every night advertising her toothpaste on television.

It felt like she hugged me even harder when I added, "If you only knew, Aunt Colette,

how much I was hoping for a little word of encouragement from you. Because if there's anyone on this earth who can understand me, it has to be you. Because you must have suffered through Aunt Beatrice's making fun of you, too. Aunt Beatrice and the others! And the whole neighbourhood! The whole world, until you finally got your role on television!"

Tears were running down her cheeks, as if someone had turned on a faucet, when I finally announced that I had given up, forever, the idea of becoming the best tap-dancer in North America! That it was too hard! That I'd decided to become what everyone wanted, a miserable veterinarian!

I think I was crying, too, when she said, "You know, sweetness, it's precisely because of my toothpaste ads on television that I didn't dare encourage you ..."

And because she felt that I finally understood her, she explained that an artist's life is not always rosy! That there were never many people in the audience to applaud her good roles! And too many people wanted to talk about the nonsense on television!

I think we would have gone on complaining forever if Aunt Alice hadn't called from downstairs to tell us our cream of mushroom soup was turning to stone in our bowls, and that both of us might have to go without chocolate pudding!

Well, I swear, it was my six other aunts who turned to stone when they saw us walk into the dining room, our eyes all red and puffy, looking so close and in cahoots together.

I hardly said a word throughout the whole meal. Neither did Aunt Colette, for that matter. It was Aunt Florence and Aunt Elisabeth who had a fight about the so-called scientific veracity of the Chinese horoscope and the horoscope in general. I usually have a ball listening to them attack each other. But this time, I was too preoccupied.

I was thinking about everything I had
lost over the past ten days. It seemed to me
that I'd have to take drastic measures and
put an end to my big dream, once and for

all. I'd have to take really drastic measures that would bring me back to earth, so that things could return to the way they were before, when I was just like everyone else. When I had lots of friends. And my hero.

I was watching Aunt Alice cut her ham when I finally realized exactly what had to be done.

After supper, I went upstairs and spent no more than a minute and a half cutting you-know-what out of the rubber soles of my running shoes. It was a minute and a half with only one witness — a half-moon that no longer looked remotely like a movie spot-light.

Now I have six big holes in my shoes and an empty ache in my heart. It's an ache so great that I closed my bedroom curtains tight last night. I didn't want to see the thousands of little lights twinkling around the moon, like thousands of future stars.

Chapter 7
Doors and Revelations

At school today, neither the principal nor any of my teachers mentioned my skipping school yesterday afternoon. I guess they were much too busy organizing the mini-Olympics in the schoolyard.

Today wasn't your usual school day. In the middle of all the mini-Olympics excitement, I ran into Marise Cormier, Marco Tifo and Julie Morin several times but didn't have a moment to say a word to them. I was looking everywhere for Pierre-Yves Hamel, when I remembered that I hadn't seen him in the schoolyard yesterday either.

Come to think of it, I hadn't seen him at all since I had returned his sweatshirt, his Swatch watch and his love letters. And when I really thought about it, I realized that my holy horror of a package on his doorstep must have made him sick! A hero is so delicate! I've known that ever since we went on vacation together in the States!

I ALMOST skipped school twice in the same week … but I didn't. I forced myself to wait until all the medals had been distributed, then I raced home and pounced on the phone.

As I dialled Pierre-Yves' number, my heart was beating so fast I thought it would explode. Then, at the other end of the line, I heard his voice. It was him! My hero! I took a deep breath.

"It's me, Rosalie," I said. "I have something important to tell you."

And without waiting for him to react, I launched into my speech: "I realize now how important I am to you. How much you must have missed me for the past ten days! But you didn't have to get sick, like some holy hopping horrible girl, because, actually, nothing has changed between us."

I also told him that I had definitely abandoned my big dream, JUST FOR HIM! That my tap-dancing days were truly over! That I was going to become a veterinarian, the way he'd always hoped I would. And if he really wanted me to, I'd go over to his house immediately and happily take back his *Swatch* watch, his sweatshirt and all his love letters!

I still had two or three things to tell him, when Pierre-Yves cut me off.

"Have you finished telling me all this nonsense, Rosalie Dansereau? I'm just having an allergic reaction to the paint. It could happen to anybody, you know. Anybody who has a mother who can't make up her mind."

And as I listened to my hero explain how the doors in his dear mother's apartment had gone from bottle green to flat white … from flat white to canary yellow … and from canary yellow back to dark bottle green, I turned as red as a beet. And I didn't even pass through the tomato-red phase, I'm sure.

There I was talking to him about love, and he, the holy horror of a heartless creep, was talking to me about kitchen doors. I couldn't help myself. Even though I hadn't heard his voice for days, I slammed the phone down on his ear. Bang!

Then I sat there wishing I hadn't returned all his things at once. Returning another little package would have made me feel a lot better.

After what felt like ages, the phone finally rang. I ran back down the hall. I grabbed the receiver, and, at the other end of the line, it was him again. He was still my hero.

"It's Pierre-Yves," he said. "Could you please let me finish what I have to say. I have something important to tell you, too."

Then, as if his allergic reaction had af-
fected his brain, he said, "You were right to
return my things to me. Because of what I'm
about to admit and what you probably already

suspected, it's very possible that you might never want to see me again."

My hero proceeded to admit something I never would have imagined. He admitted that THE PERSON WHO CARED ABOUT ME WAS HIM! And that, at the time, he hadn't realized how cowardly he was being. I had been making it impossible for anyone to approach me!

But now, he really understood why I acted the way I did with him. I was such an honest, direct person! I had all the reason in the world to avoid someone who was cowardly enough to send an anonymous letter!

"The only thing I don't understand, Rosalie Dansereau," he said, "is the note you wrote on the package! First of all, you are still the one I care about ... And I can't think of anyone who would look better in my sweatshirt than you."

So, for the first time since I learned how to babble, I didn't know what to say. This was the first time I had ever been left speechless, with my mouth hanging open so wide I could have swallowed all the black flies in the province of Quebec.

It was also the first time that I've ever hung up on someone without really meaning to. I mean, the receiver just slipped out of my hand. Almost as if it had become much too heavy for me to hold. Phew!

After Pierre-Yves' telephone call, I tried for the second time that week to convince my aunts that we absolutely had to move from the neighbourhood as soon as possible. But since nobody ever tries to understand anything in this house … I had to go back to St. Mary's School the following morning. Even though I was ashamed! Really ashamed! So ashamed that I could die!

It must have rained all night, because there were puddles of water up and down the sidewalks. But I couldn't have cared less about the water that came streaming through the six holes in my shoes. I pretended that my running shoes were two German submarines sinking to the bottom of the ocean.

No wonder! I was purposely walking through all the puddles, and the water was pouring in through the six open portholes.

I tried to convince myself that if I stayed hidden behind my dark glasses and concentrated on wartime submersibles, I would forget the holy hopping horror of an anonymous letter I had written, by mistake, to my best friend.

I thought that if I could stay hidden, I'd stop worrying about the day when Pierre-Yves Hamel would find out all about it — the day when it would be my turn to receive a big package containing my wool scarf, my cat figurine, my four you-are-the-hero books and all my love letters.

But when I walked into the schoolyard, I was still as worried as ever. Even worse, I was racking my brains trying to find some way to tell Julie Morin she wasn't the person I had thought she was.

I had to find some way of telling her that she wasn't really a plotting, hypocritical, sneaky, jealous, pretentious gossip. There had to be some way of telling her that, actually, she wasn't at all the typical Scorpio-Snake described in Auntie Flo's books!

I still hadn't found a solution when the person I had unfairly insulted in ten long pages walked over to me.

Deadly serious, she asked, "Rosalie Dansereau, could you please tell me why we don't see you practicing anymore?"

And without skipping a beat, she went on, "I'm not kidding. Towards the end, your flaps, your shim shams and your triple time steps, even your wings and your pullbacks, were getting pretty good!"

It's dumb, but I just melted, melted, melted. Gradually. Like a quart of ice cream that had landed in a microwave by mistake.

I still couldn't make head nor tail of her

gobbledygook, but you don't always have to understand every word to know when someone is complimenting you! Encouraging you! Saying they like you!

I hoped, from the bottom of my heart, that my best friend hadn't figured everything out. That's what I hoped, but I didn't know what to think when she came so close that only I could hear her, and said, "You know, Rosalie Dansereau, I don't believe in the Chinese horoscope or in any other horoscope anymore."

And, believe me, I was absolutely, totally lost when she added, "It's all because of the exact time of your birth!"

Then my best friend proceeded to explain that, according to her latest calculations, I should have been nothing but a handful of putty, the marshmallow type, who never took any initiatives of her own, and spent her life imitating others! A description which, she felt, had nothing to do with reality!

Furthermore, she felt that when a theory is in total opposition to reality, it can only mean that the theory isn't scientifically sound! Therefore, astrology was nothing but hogwash!

In other words, my best friend dared admit to me: "Actually, I always knew that you had both the talent and the hardheadedness it takes to become a big star. And to prove it, you already have a fan club."

Then, to prove her point, Julie Morin pulled me by the sleeve and led me over to the other side of the schoolyard.

On the way, she told me my biggest fan's name was Leona Lafleur. When we arrived on the other side, I immediately recognized the little girl from grade two who had repeated after Julie: "We liked you better when you wanted to take care of sick cats and dogs and pigeons."

But now, little Leona was facing the school wall and she, too, was dancing! As I watched her dance and dance and dance, I recognized every step, every single move from the grand finale of the best movie Fred Astaire ever made.

When Leona finally stopped dancing, she turned around and her face lit up. She looked like she wanted to touch me, but didn't dare.

She simply said, a bit shyly, "My dream is to become as good as you some day!"

Then, she picked up her feet, one after the other, and showed me the soles of her shoes.

"You see, I have six of them, stuck on with *Crazy Glue*, just like you!"

It's silly, but I just stood there. I was too stunned, too moved, too surprised to say anything. Finally, I raised my sunglasses and smiled at her.

I think I was still smiling when Julie Morin, without consulting me or anything, suggested, "I bet Rosalie would be happy to give you some lessons."

At that point, I'm sure I stopped smiling. Me give someone lessons! Wait a minute! My friend Julie was getting a bit carried away!

Then I thought about my pierced submarines. And the more I thought about the holes in my clodhoppers, the harder the little girl tugged on my T-shirt, almost begging me.

Finally, I answered, in spite of myself, "We can start next week, if you want."

The schoolbell began to clang. It was a good thing, too, because Leona Lafleur had begun to insist that we start our lessons right then and there.

Phew, that was a narrow escape — or so I thought. I entered the classroom, convinced that neither Leona nor my best friend had noticed anything unusual about the soles of my shoes. But the minute she sat down at her desk, Julie Morin turned around and asked, loudly enough for everyone to hear, "What's the big idea, Rosalie Dansereau? Why did you make those holes in your shoes?"

I don't know what came over me, but just so she wouldn't think that I'm the holy

horrible Gemini-Horse I really am, I whispered in her ear: "It's all Aunt Beatrice's fault! She's the one who forced me to cut up my shoes! She said I was ruining her floors!"

Julie Morin knows Sergeant Celery very well.

"I always knew that your Aunt Beatrice could be difficult," she whispered back.

Without batting an eyelash, I continued like the worst coward, the worst liar, the worst *twister* of truth in the world. "Difficult," I gasped. "Difficult! That's putting it mildly. Aunt Beatrice is a MONSTER!"

After that, it was hopeless. I couldn't concentrate on wartime submersibles, and I couldn't pay attention in class, either. I spent almost the entire holy hopping horrible day thinking about either Pierre-Yves Hamel or Julie Morin or Beatrice Dansereau.

There are nights, holy hopping horrible nights, when it's impossible to fall asleep. Even if it's two o'clock in the morning. Even if you are tucked into your own bed.

The reason I can't fall asleep tonight is not because I am the worst liar, the worst hypocrite and the biggest coward on earth. It's not because Pierre-Yves Hamel still believes that I'm an honest, direct person! Or because, next Monday morning, little Leona will be waiting at school for her first tap-dancing lesson!

Nor is it because Marise Cormier phoned to offer me her old pair of shoes. Or because Marco Tifo called and invited me to practice in his garage. It's not even because my seven aunts have just enrolled me in the best dance school in Quebec. Or because Aunt Beatrice just gave me, with certain restrictions, of course, the most beautiful pair of tap shoes, complete with taps and everything.

No, the reason I can't fall asleep is because I just finished writing the longest, the thickest, the most enormous anonymous letter ever written.

Believe me, it was no piece of cake copying all, absolutely all, the positive characteristics, not only of Scorpio-Snakes, but of all the signs of the Chinese horoscope and horoscopes in general from Auntie Flo's books.

It came to thirty-three holy hopping pages in all! Thirty-three holy hopping horrible pages of compliments strung together!

And now I can't fall asleep because I can hardly wait to slip it into her desk tomorrow! I can hardly wait to see Julie Morin read, and reread, that in times of great catastrophe, the most dependable friends are definitely scorpio-snakes.

I can hardly wait to see her turn around and say to me, "This is without a doubt the most beautiful anonymous letter I've ever received, Rosalie Dansereau!"

Maybe then I'll be able to take back my hero's sweatshirt, his *Swatch* watch and all his love letters. Maybe someday I'll have the courage to admit to him that I, too, once had an uncontrollable urge to write a letter to someone without signing it. A thirty-three page letter, to be precise.

Just as there are nights when it's impossible to fall asleep, there are days when you feel like kissing everyone. Days when forty-two pairs of dark glasses would still let the tiniest ray of sun shine through.

Days when you don't have the slightest

desire to move, to change friends or neighbourhoods. Days when you are not the least
bit discouraged about being brought up by
seven mothers.

There are days when you are sure you
have almost everything it takes to become
the greatest video clip tap-dancer on St.
Joseph Boulevard. And in North America.
And maybe even Europe and Asia, too.

So, even if there are nights when, at two
o'clock in the morning, you still can't fall

asleep ... you're so happy, so hopeful, that you feel as if you are already in a dream! And it's a dream where your best friend tells everyone the most holy hopping horribly nice things about you.

It's unbelievable how well I know my best friend, Julie.

To prove it, the next day, everything happened exactly the way I hoped it would. At least, almost everything.

After she read, and reread, my thirty-three pages, she had to add, "You're crazy, Rosalie Dansereau. Ten pages, like the other letter, would have been enough. Really!"

It's also unbelievable how much I'm learning at the best dance school in Quebec.

Not only am I learning how to make my feet talk, I'm also learning to understand all the gobbledygook.

I mean, now I know that flap, pullback, shim sham, Irish time step, wing, travelling, riff, brush and shuffle are the real names for certain dance steps, certain movements or a certain series of steps.

I also know that I have a long way to go if I want to become as good as Fred Astaire. But that's not a problem anymore. Now there are twelve of us soul mates who practice like crazy in the schoolyard. We no longer rehearse you-know-who's grand finale, but an original dance we made up ourselves.

It's for the school Christmas show. And even though we can all hardly wait to twirl our canes and wear our top hats and sequined costumes — even though we can hardly wait to tap our feet, to jump and slide and spin around like twelve superstars — sometimes I feel a bit scared.

I'm afraid I might trip like some holy horrible beginner. I'm afraid someone might throw a pail of water at me — or a tomato, a potato, a turnip or a rotten egg.

Julie Morin says I let my imagination run away with me. After everything that has happened lately, I hope that, with her holy hopping horrible intelligence, she'll turn out to be right, as usual.

About the Author

Ginette Anfousse was born in Montreal and has been an artist all her life. She started out as a ballet dancer, then worked as an illustrator for television, magazines and newspapers, and eventually began writing children's books. She created the popular Rosalie Series after receiving encouragement from her many readers over the years.

Ginette Anfousse's awards as an author and illustrator include the coveted Mr. Christie Book Award and a nomination for the Governor-General's Literary Award. Her work has received international recognition.

About the Illustrator

Marisol Sarrazin was born in Sainte-Agathe-des-Monts, Quebec, and studied graphic design in Montreal. She is a dynamic and talented artist who enjoys working in many different fields in the visual and performing arts, but her first love is drawing.

The Rosalie Series is an appropriate project for Marisol Sarrazin —as Ginette Anfousse's daughter, she not only illustrated the fictional characters, she was also the inspiration for some of them!

MORE GREAT BOOKS IN THE ROSALIE SERIES!

Meet Rosalie, who is exactly nine years, seven months and three days old ... and has exactly seven mothers. Aided by her lively gang of friends and her cat Charcoal, Rosalie embarks on a series of hilarious, not-to-be-missed adventures.

"A fun first chapter book that takes a fresh and, at times, outrageous look at life in a non-traditional family. Rosalie is an engaging protagonist, and her first-person narration gives the story a sense of exuberant energy." *Quill & Quire*

ISBN 0-921556-47-0
$5.95 paperback (not available in the USA)
ISBN 0-921556-49-7
$10.95 hardcover

The Rosalie Series

by Ginette Anfousse
Illustrated by Marisol Sarrazin
Translated by Linda Gaboriau

Rosalie is back! And so are her seven mothers, her two cats and her gang of friends. This time, her adventure begins when a schoolyard snowball fight turns sour and becomes "war." While Rosalie learns some truths about real war from the Vietnamese immigrant Piam Low, her new kitten goes missing and her friend Pierre-Yves is hospitalized with pneumonia. Will Rosalie's battles never end? Find out how Rosalie's busy life unfolds, in this second irresistible book in the series.

ISBN 0-921556-50-0
$5.95 paperback (not available in the USA)

ISBN 0-921556-51-9
$10.95 hardcover

MORE BOOKS BY RAGWEED PRESS

Next Teller
A Book of Canadian Storytelling
Collected by Dan Yashinsky

Thirty-one Canadian storytellers from various cultural backgrounds and regions have contributed to this spellbinding collection of stories about love, wisdom and change.

"... while [the storytellers] will probably be forgotten, their stories will be remembered." *Quill & Quire*

"In *Next Teller* ... there are some [stories] that jump off the page dying to be told." *Globe and Mail*

ISBN 0-921556-46-2   **$12.95**

The Storyteller at Fault
Dan Yashinsky
Illustrated by Nancy Cairine Pitt

A masterful tale of adventure, wit and suspense, by an accomplished raconteur. Folk literature and oral traditions from around the world are woven into a colourful tapestry that is a whole new tale in itself.

ISBN 0-921556-29-2   **$9.95**

Dan Yashinsky is a well-known storyteller who lives in Toronto. He regularly practises his craft at storytelling festivals, in schools and anywhere he can find a listener.

RAGWEED
THE ISLAND PUBLISHER

Mogul and Me

Peter Cumming
Illustrated by P. John Burden

Based on a true story, this dramatic tale of the friendship between a New Brunswick farmboy and a circus elephant is also a story of love and trust, and good and evil.

ISBN 0-920304-82-6 **$8.95**

Bigfoot Sabotage

Deirdre Kessler

"Deirdre Kessler has woven an exciting tale combining the actualities of clearcut logging, the pros and cons of which are stated simply and fairly, with a more mythic story of the sasquatch. Kessler's descriptions of western mountain meadow land and forest are superb, and her characters are a spunky pair." *Monica Hughes*, award-winning children's book author

ISBN 0-921556-19-5 **$6.95**

RAGWEED PRESS books can be found in quality bookstores, or individual orders may be sent prepaid to: RAGWEED PRESS, P.O. Box 2023, Charlottetown, Prince Edward Island, Canada, C1A 7N7. Please add postage and handling ($3.00 for the first book and 75 cents for each additional book) to your order. Canadian residents add 7% GST to the total amount. GST registration number R104383120.